The First Morning
AN AFRICAN MYTH

▼▼

Retold by **Margery Bernstein and Janet Kobrin**

Illustrated by **Enid Warner Romanek**

CHARLES SCRIBNER'S SONS ◇ NEW YORK

To
Edgar Bernstein
and
Philip Montag
whose talents created the Independent
Learning Project, and whose support and
enthusiasm made this book possible.

The First Morning was first told by the Sukuma people of East Africa.

▼▼

Printed in the United States of America
Library of Congress Catalog Card Number 75-27705
1 3 5 7 9 11 13 15 17 19 MD/C 20 18 16 14 12 10 8 6 4 2
ISBN 0-684-14533-2

The First Morning

AN AFRICAN MYTH

A very long time ago there was
no light anywhere in the world.
    It was hard for the animals
to see. They bumped into trees.
They fell into holes. In the dark
they even stumbled over each other.
    This made them very unhappy.

Finally Lion, who was king,
called a meeting.

"My friends," said Lion, "we do
not have to live in the dark.
I know where we can find light."

"Sometimes when there is a storm the sky cracks open. Above the sky I have seen light. Will someone try to bring this light to earth?"

"I will go," said Mouse.

"We will go with you," said Spider and Fly.

First they had to get up to the sky. Spider spun her web all the way up through the clouds. She spun it all the way to where the sky begins.

Then Mouse climbed up the web. She chewed a little hole in the bottom of the sky.

Spider, Fly, and Mouse climbed through to the other side.

Above the sky there was light!
All around them was a large
grassy plain. There were many sky
people cutting the grass.

They took Mouse, Spider,
and Fly to their king.

"O King," said Mouse,
"may we have some of your
light to take back to earth?"

"O Mouse," said the king, "I would like to give you some light but I must ask my people first."

But the king was selfish. He did
not really want to share the light.
So he called a meeting.
It was a long and secret meeting.

Finally, the king said,
"I know how to get rid of
those earth creatures. I will
make up a test that they
cannot pass."

"Then I will kill them."

But the king
did not know that
Fly was listening.

When the meeting was over the king said to Mouse, "There is something you must do for me. I need grass to cover the houses I am building. If you can cut all the grass on this big plain by tomorrow morning, I will give you light."

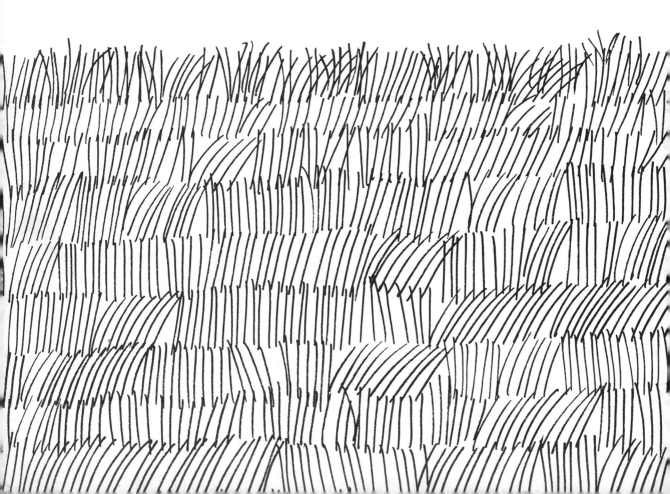

When the king had gone, Fly said to Mouse, "I was at the secret meeting. I hid, so no one saw me. The king plans to kill us if we cannot cut all the grass. What shall we do?"

Mouse thought and thought. "I have an idea," she said.

Mouse climbed down Spider's web.
When she got to earth she called all
the ants.

That night millions of ants
quietly followed Mouse up the web
into the sky. They quickly cut
all the grass on the plain.
Then they stole down the web
to earth.

In the morning, Mouse showed
the king that the work was done.
The king pretended to be
pleased but he was really angry.

"I cannot give you light yet," he said. "I must call another meeting."

"These creatures must be great and powerful," he told the sky people. "One test is not enough for them."

The king called Mouse, Spider, and Fly and said to them, "Now you must pass another test."

"I will roast a whole cow.
If you can eat all of it, I
promise I will give you light."
Then the king went away.

✺

But Fly had been at the second
meeting, too. He told Mouse and
Spider the rest of the king's plan.

"The king will kill us if we
can't eat the whole cow," Fly said.
"What are we going to do?"

"Don't worry," said Mouse.
"I know what we can do."

That evening, the sky people
brought many bowls of meat.

"Thank you," said Mouse.
"Tomorrow morning you can come
and take the empty bowls away."

When the sky people had gone,
Mouse dug long tunnels in the ground.
Then Mouse, Spider, and Fly
buried all the meat in the tunnels.

In the morning when the sky
people came the bowls were all empty!
But still the king would not keep
his promise. He had a third meeting.
Again Fly hid in the corner and listened.

The king was furious.

"We must give them some of our light," he said. "But I will make it hard for them."

"I have two boxes. The black box holds darkness. The red box holds light. They will have to choose one."

Of course Fly told Mouse which box had the light in it.

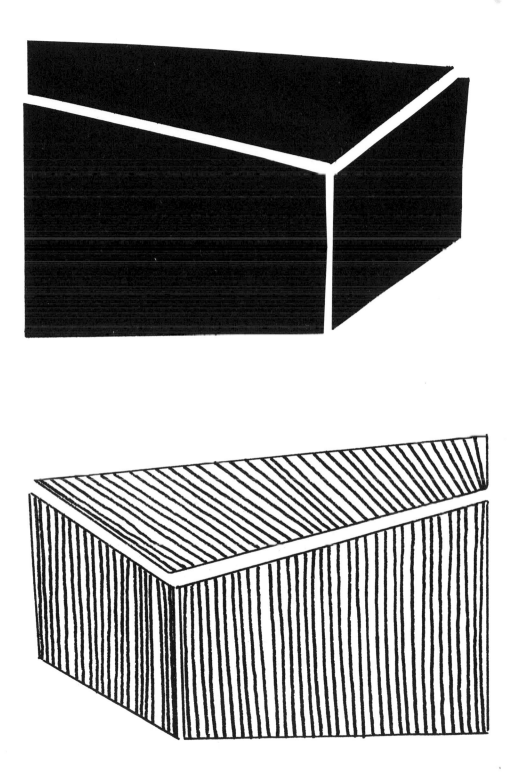

The King called Spider, Mouse,
and Fly.

"Here are two boxes," he said.
"One holds light, the other has
only darkness."

"Which one will you choose?"

"Let me see," said Mouse.
She pretended it was hard to decide.
Finally Mouse pointed to the red box.

"I think I will choose this one," she said.

Before the king could think of another trick, Mouse snatched the box and slid quickly down the web.

Back on earth all the animals
gathered around Mouse, Spider,
and Fly.

Mouse told them what had happened.
She showed them the red box.

"Open the box!" said Lion.
"Yes, open the box!" begged
the other animals.
Slowly, slowly, Mouse lifted
the lid of the box.

There was nothing in the box
but a rooster!

All the animals started to laugh.

"It's nothing but a rooster,"
said Lion.

"A rooster isn't light,"
said Leopard.

All the animals laughed at Mouse
and her box.

Poor Mouse! She was so ashamed!
She was sure she had been tricked
after all.

Then, suddenly,
the rooster jumped
out of the box.

"Cock-a-doodle-do," he crowed.

At once the sky began to glow
in the east.
"Cock-a-doodle-do,"
he crowed again.
The golden sun
burst into the sky.

There was light
on the earth for
the very first time.

The rooster had called up the sun. And he has called it up every morning from that day to this.